WHEN CAVE MEN PAINTED

WHEN CAVE MEN PAINTED

written and illustrated by NORMAN BATE

CHARLES SCRIBNER'S SONS
NEW YORK

FOR HOLLIS

Long, long ago, when the world was different than it is now, wild and big and fierce animals roamed the land . . .

And people lived in caves.

The people were not as big or strong as the great wild animals. Their only weapons were stone axes and stone-tipped spears.

So they lived together and hunted together in order to protect themselves.

And they put their faith in the power of magic performed by an old man of the tribe, a magic that came from animal pictures he painted on the cave walls.

One day in those times, a boy sat quietly on the side of a steep hill and watched the valley below. He knew that animals would come out of the forest to bathe or drink at the river's edge.

He might see a huge bison or a cave bear or a powerful aurochs. He might see a shaggy boar or a reindeer or swift and small wild horses.

He knew these animals well. He had seen them in the old man's paintings on the walls of the magic cave.

The boy saw something move at the river's edge.

Several wild bison came out of the forest. They were too big for him to hunt alone. He would go back to his tribe and tell the hunters. They would plan the hunt.

He moved noiselessly up the hill and ran swiftly toward the cave of his people.

Suddenly, he stopped.

A huge and terrible animal blocked his path.

It had two long, sharp horns on the end of its nose—one behind the other.

Its skin was heavy and wrinkled and hairy.

Its eyes were small and black and unblinking.

The boy trembled with fear. He had not seen paintings of this animal in the magic cave.

The beast charged!
Its great pounding feet shook the earth!

The boy turned and fled. He jumped over rocks and boulders, leaped across crevices, and ran where the great beast could not follow.

It snorted loudly, then turned away toward the river.

The boy arrived breathless and shaking at the cave of his people. He spoke wildly to the hunters about the great new beast he had seen. He told them of its size and its eyes, of its skin and its two sharp horns—one behind the other!

This was an animal the hunters had never seen.

And they were afraid.

Then the boy looked for the old man. He crawled down into
the deep, winding passages of the magic cave.

Hundreds of animal paintings covered the cave walls.

There were bison and aurochs and huge black bulls, red reindeer and brown horses and little yellow ponies.

In the paintings each animal seemed alive—running or jumping or falling with a spear in its side.

The boy found the old man sitting by a small fire at the end of the cave. He told him about the terrible animal.

The old man listened—and sat silent for many minutes.

This was an animal that was strange to him. It was not among his paintings, nor among those done by other painters before him. He did not wish to believe the boy, but . . .

He, too, was afraid.

Then he spoke. He told the boy that only the magic of a great new painting would make them unafraid.

He would need fresh paints and new brushes to work with, and sharp stone tools to scratch lines in the rock.

He would need many lamps to see by and a high, strong platform from which to paint.

He told the boy to get all these things.

The boy went back to the hunters. He told them that a platform was needed.

They went to the forest and cut straight, young trees with their stone axes. The trimmed trunks were dragged one by one down the twisting passages of the cave. Then they lashed the poles together with strips of leather.

And a strong platform was made.

The boy gathered dish-shaped stones and filled them with melted animal fat. Into each dish of fat he placed a wick made from the shredded inner bark of trees. He carried these lamps into the cave and lit them.

Then the boy asked the hunters for their stone knives. He chose the best and the sharpest, and gave them to the old man.

The old man climbed up on the platform and began to cut an outline of the great new animal into the soft rock of the cave wall.

While the old man worked, the boy went to the river bank
and dug out pieces of dry clay. The clay was of many colors—
red and yellow and brown and gray.

He kept all the colors separate and ground each piece of
clay between two flat stones until he had many different piles
of colored dust.

Then he mixed each pile with melted animal fat to make a
brilliant liquid paint. He poured the paints into hollow
bones to keep them fresh and moist.

The boy gathered wax from the hives of wild bees and mixed it with other colored dusts. He rolled each waxy mixture between his hands to make thick, crayon-like colored sticks.

The old man needed brushes. Some of these the boy made by tying tufts of animal hair to the ends of twigs. Some he made by shredding the ends of fibrous plants.

Then the boy carried all the bones filled with paint and the brushes and the crayons down into the magic cave where the old man worked.

He stood at the base of the platform and listened.

The old man was chanting magic words.

The boy had been told that the magic of the chanted words could travel through earth and sky. It would reach the frightening new animal and make it less fierce. It would reach the hunters and make them strong and cunning and successful in their hunt.

He knew that he must learn these strange and mysterious words.

Then the boy looked at the outline of the fierce animal the old man had carved.

It did not look like the huge and frightening animal he had seen.

He tried to say so—but the old man would not listen.

The boy was afraid.

He helped the old man in fearful silence. He made black paint by mixing soot from the fires and melted fat from the lamps.

The old man used the black paint to brush broad and heavy strokes over the carved outline of the new animal. He forced the paint deep into the grain of the rock.

When the painted outline of the animal was finished, he used the colored wax sticks to draw wrinkles and folds in the heavy skin. Then he used the yellow and red paints to make the markings on its body. Finally, he used the dark colors to make the shadows and give the animal roundness.

The boy watched and listened—for the old man never stopped chanting his magic words.

The finished painting was very large. It showed an animal that could shake the earth—or rip a man apart with its two sharp nose horns.

The boy looked at it, and he looked at the paintings of
other animals on the walls.

The new beast did not have the smoothness and grace of
the wild horses or the small ponies nearby.

Nor did it have the patterns and markings of the great bulls, nor the beauty and delicacy of the fine reindeer that ran together between the great bulls.

It was round and real and frightening, but it did not look like the beast the boy had seen!

He was fearful that the magic of the old man's chant would fail.

Then the hunters came into the magic cave. The platform and paints and tools were taken away. Small fires were lit. The old man put on a bird-like mask and a fine robe made of feathers and fur. He held a magic staff that had a carved wooden bird at its top.

The hunters began to sing and chant and dance. Their moving bodies cast weird shadows on the wall. Each man touched the new painting with his spear.

They thought that the old man's magic would flow from the painting into their spears and give them great strength and skill for the hunt.

The old man, too, chanted and danced. Then he left the cave and walked out into the night. He climbed the highest hill and stood there with his masked face raised toward the stars.

He asked the unknown gods to let his magic fly out over the valley and out over the mysterious new beast that was frightening his people.

When the hunters had finished their ritual dance, it was dawn and they had great courage.

Swiftly, while their magic was still strong, they left the cave and the boy led them to the place where he had met the frightening beast.

But they found no strange new animal.

All day they searched.

They saw many animals, but not the one they hunted. And when the great bison and aurochs and bulls crossed their path, they let them go. For to kill any other animal would weaken the magic in their spears.

As the sun began to set, they heard loud noises coming from the river's edge.

Animals bellowed and snorted!

Trees crashed down!

The ground shook!

Then all was quiet. Cautiously, the boy and the hunters approached the river. Their spears were ready.

What they saw made them stop.

A great bison stood in the center of a trampled clearing.
Its side was ripped open. The bison swayed weakly and its
head drooped almost to the ground.

At its feet lay the old man, still dressed in bird mask and
robes of feather and fur. The magic staff with its carved bird
lay near his lifeless hand.

And walking away from the old man and the dying bison was a huge rhinoceros. Its great double horns were covered with blood and fur.

The rhinoceros looked like no animal that the hunters had ever seen, nor did it look like the one in the old man's painting.

But the boy knew that this was the strange beast he had faced before!

The hunters hurled their sharp spears at the great rhinoceros. Their weapons flew straight and true . . .

But they bounced off the animal's thick hide and fell harmlessly to the ground. The old man's magic had failed.

The hunters were once more afraid.

The beast snorted and walked slowly away. It disappeared in the thick forest along the river's edge.

When the beast had gone, the hunters carefully picked up the old man and carried him back to his cave.

He was taken to the farthest corner and buried at the bottom of a deep and narrow pit.

Then the boy knew that *he* must protect his people.

He gathered together all of the tools and brushes and paints, he thought of all the magic words, and he began to paint on the wall above the old man's grave.

The hunters watched. They listened to his chant.

Suddenly, they were no longer afraid.

For the boy painted a picture of the battle they had seen at the river's edge—the bison with its side gashed open, the old man in his bird-like costume lying on the ground, and the great woolly rhinoceros walking away.

The hunters gained courage. They knew that the boy's painting of the rhinoceros was true.

It looked exactly like the strange new animal they had seen.

From that day on, the boy became the painter of the cave until he, too, was an old, old man . . .

And the men of the tribe were able to hunt without fear.

All of this happened more than twenty thousand years ago, but the paintings of the bison, the aurochs, the horses, the bulls, and the old man and the rhinoceros can be seen today.

They are among hundreds of animal paintings high on the walls and ceilings in the cave of Lascaux in France.